Reindeer of the Arctic

Heather Rising

Contents

What Are Reindeer?

Reindeer are a kind of deer.
Many reindeer live near the **Arctic Circle** in the northern parts of Europe and North America. In North America, reindeer are called caribou (say: *ca-ri-boo*).

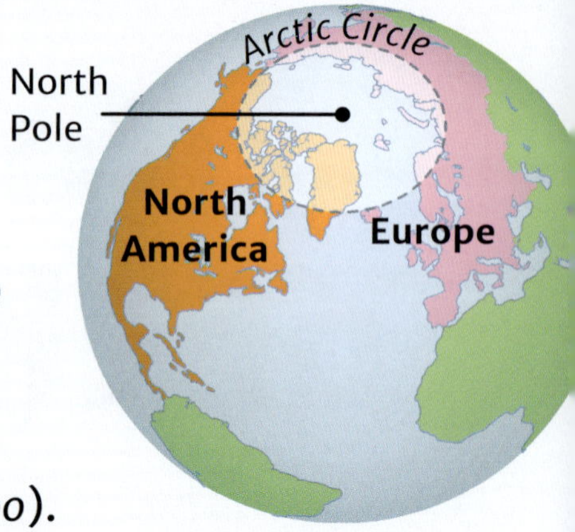

North
Pole
Arctic Circle
North America
Europe

The Arctic Circle is the land and sea around the North Pole.

Reindeer live in herds. They can form huge groups of thousands of animals in spring. These herds **migrate**, or move, thousands of kilometres each year to find food.

This view from above shows a reindeer herd in the Arctic Circle.

The hair on reindeer can be different colours, from dark brown to grey. The hair of some reindeer changes to white in winter.

The hair of the Peary caribou turns white in winter.

Reindeer have two layers of hair. The layer closest to their skin is soft and fluffy. The layer on the outside is longer and rougher. A reindeer's hair helps to protect it from freezing temperatures.

A reindeer's layers of hair keep it warm.

When standing, a male reindeer is around 1.4 metres high at the shoulder. Males are bigger and heavier than females, and can weigh over 200 kilograms.

Reindeer grow new **antlers** each year.
The antlers can be over a metre tall.
Both male and female reindeer grow antlers.
In other types of deer, only the males grow antlers.

Male reindeer are usually bigger than female reindeer.

Most reindeer have long legs that help them to run well. Their hooves are very wide. This helps reindeer to walk on snow without sinking. Reindeer are good swimmers and can cross large lakes. They use their hooves like paddles.

The bottom of a reindeer's hoof is shaped like an upside-down letter "U".

Reindeer hooves change with the seasons. In spring, the hooves are softer to help stop the reindeer from sinking into icy ground as the ice melts. In winter, the hooves harden so that the reindeer can use them to dig through snow to find food.

Reindeer hooves work like snowshoes. They help the reindeer walk over the top of deep snow.

Reindeer use their hooves to find food under the snow.

Habitat and Food

Reindeer spend the summer months near the Arctic Circle, in an area called the **tundra**.

Only the top 10 centimetres of ground in the tundra melts in summer. The deeper ground stays frozen all year. This means that trees cannot grow in the tundra. Only grasses, flowering plants and small bushes grow there. Reindeer eat the plants that they can find.

Reindeer graze on plants in the tundra.

In winter, reindeer migrate south. Female reindeer lead this migration. The reindeer return to the same place each year – an area where the snow is less deep and there are plenty of plants. They dig down into the snow and scrape moss and **lichens** off rocks to eat. Some herds spend time in the mountains or woodlands where they also eat small trees.

Reindeer must keep moving and cover great distances to find enough food. Each reindeer needs to eat about 7 kilograms of food a day. Some herds travel 5000 kilometres a year. Reindeer droppings provide important **nutrients** to the tundra plants in the areas where the reindeer walk.

In winter, reindeer move to areas where there is more food.

Life Cycle

Reindeer **mate** in autumn. Their calves are born about seven to eight months later, in late spring or early summer. Calves can stand soon after they are born. Then, after only a few hours, they can run. A calf drinks its mother's milk until it is around five months old, but it starts to graze after a few weeks.

A reindeer calf is able to run not long after it is born.

The young calves must be able to follow the herd. And they must be able to escape from predators, such as wolves and bears.

This reindeer calf needs to keep up with its mother as they cross a river.

Each year, reindeer grow a new set of antlers. Male reindeer begin to grow theirs in early spring. Female reindeer's antlers start growing in late spring or early summer, usually after they have their calves.

Reindeer antlers look like bony branches.

While reindeer antlers are growing, they are covered with a fur called **velvet**. When the antlers are fully grown and have hardened, the velvet falls off.

Reindeer antlers that are covered in velvet are still growing.

Male reindeer use their antlers to battle other males for females. They **shed** their antlers in the winter months.

Female reindeer use their antlers to defend food they find. They usually shed their antlers when their calves are still young.

Two reindeer use their antlers to fight each other.

Reindeer and People

For thousands of years, people have hunted wild reindeer. In the past, reindeer were very important for some people's survival. **Indigenous peoples** from around the Arctic Circle ate reindeer meat and used the skins to make warm clothing and shelters. They made tools from the bones and antlers.

The Inuit word for caribou is "tuktu" (say: *tuk-too*).

Clothing made from reindeer skins keeps these Inuit children warm.

Over time, people in the Arctic areas of Europe and Asia began to keep reindeer close to them. They stopped the reindeer from migrating too far so that hunting them would be easier. There are still wild herds of reindeer in these countries, but now there are rules about hunting them.

These farmers in Europe keep reindeer for their milk.

Today, some reindeer are kept on farms. Most people now buy farmed reindeer meat to eat, instead of hunting them.

Inuit (say: *In-yoo-it*) peoples live in the Arctic areas of North America. They are one group of Indigenous peoples who still rely on hunting wild caribou to feed their communities.

Some Indigenous peoples use reindeer for transport.

Today, many humans live and work in areas where reindeer live. People have found oil and minerals inside the Arctic Circle. There are now huge pipelines above the ground for moving oil, and highways to get people to the mines. Reindeer must travel across large areas to find enough to eat, but often their migration pathways are blocked by roads and pipelines.

Crossing roads can be dangerous for reindeer.

This huge pipeline was built through a reindeer habitat.

Building roads and laying pipelines damages reindeer habitats. It also drives other animals into the areas where reindeer live. That means more animals must try to find food in smaller areas. And more predators move into the places where reindeer have their calves, so the young reindeer are in greater danger.

Reindeer in a Changing Environment

Global temperatures are rising due to **climate change**. This means that spring now begins earlier in the Arctic. When reindeer calves are old enough to eat plants, the plants are already fully grown and too tough for the calves to chew. The bigger plants are also not as healthy for the adults. Reindeer may not get enough good food to eat.

Reindeer need to be strong enough to swim across large lakes.

Reindeer often need to swim across large lakes when they migrate. When frozen lakes melt too early, the reindeer may begin their migration across the lakes too soon. Their calves are still too little, and not strong enough to make the long swim.

Rising temperatures mean that freezing rain falls, instead of snow. This leaves moss, lichens and small plants coated in hard ice that the reindeer cannot break through to reach their food.

The effects of climate change make it harder for reindeer to find food.

An earlier spring means that clouds of blood-sucking insects appear at the same time reindeer calves are born. An adult reindeer can lose almost 2 kilograms of blood to biting insects in a year. These insects can cover a whole calf, making it weak.

The lives of reindeer calves can be put at risk by blood-sucking mosquitoes.

Helping Reindeer

Today, the number of reindeer in each herd is falling. Reindeer live for around five years in the wild – their **lifespans** are not long. If too few calves are born year after year, a herd can be reduced to almost nothing.

It is important for scientists to track reindeer numbers. They can photograph herds from planes. Their research can help make laws to stop the reindeer from being hunted too much.

Scientists collect blood from a reindeer to use for research.

Scientists keep track of reindeer by putting signal collars on them. **Satellites** are used to follow the reindeer on their migration pathways. This information is used to help decide where to build roads and new developments.

A reindeer wears a signal collar so its movements can be tracked.

The Arctic National Wildlife Refuge in Alaska, USA is protected land. A herd of Porcupine caribou uses the area to have its calves. This herd is healthy and has almost 200 000 animals.

Reindeer are an important part of the environment in the Arctic. They are food for wolves and bears, and their droppings keep the plants in the tundra healthy.

Reindeer live in, and cross into, different countries when they migrate. Not every country has the same laws for protecting reindeer.

Governments can do things to help reindeer. Pipelines can be buried underground in areas where reindeer roam. Wildlife bridges can be built for animals to cross highways and roads safely.

We all need to work together to protect reindeer and the environment where they live.

Glossary

antlers (*noun*) bony growths on a reindeer's head that look like tree branches

Arctic Circle (*proper noun*) an imaginary circle around the most northern part of Earth

climate change (*noun*) a change in weather patterns around the world

Indigenous peoples (*proper noun*) the first peoples living in an area

lichens (*noun*) slow-growing, crusty plants that grow on rocks and trees

lifespans (*noun*) the lengths of time that living things survive

mate (*verb*) to come together to produce babies

migrate (*verb*) to move from one region to another due to a change of season

nutrients (*noun*) fats, vitamins, proteins and other things found in food and soil that help a plant or animal live and grow

satellites (*noun*) objects sent into space to orbit around a planet

shed (*verb*) to lose body parts, like antlers or hair, because they are old or no longer needed

tundra (*noun*) a very cold area with hard, rocky, frozen ground where trees do not grow

velvet (*noun*) the soft, furry covering on an antler

Index